ER 792.78 THO
Thomas, Mark,
Tap dancing / by Mark
Thomas.

Let's Dance

FOUNTAINDALE PUBLIC LIBRARY DISTRICT
300 West Briarcliff Road
Bolingbrook, IL 60440-2894
(630) 759-2102

Tap Dancing

By Mark Thomas

Children's Press
A Division of Grolier Publishing
New York / London / Hong Kong / Sydney
Danbury, Connecticut

Thanks to the students of the Broadway Bound Dance Academy

Photo Credits: Cover and all photos by Maura Boruchow
Contributing Editor: Jeri Cipriano
Book Design: Christopher Logan

Visit Children's Press on the Internet at:
http://publishing.grolier.com

Library of Congress Cataloging-in-Publication Data

Thomas, Mark, 1963-
Tap dancing / by Mark Thomas.
p. cm. — (Let's dance)
Includes bibliographical references and index.
ISBN 0-516-23146-4 (lib. bdg.) — ISBN 0-516-23071-9 (pbk.)
1. Tap dancing—Juvenile literature. [1. Tap dancing.] I. Title.

GV1794 .T56 2000
792.7'8—dc21

00-043184

Copyright © 2001 by Rosen Book Works, Inc.
All rights reserved. Published simultaneously in Canada.
Printed in the United States of America.
1 2 3 4 5 6 7 8 9 10 R 05 04 03 02 01

Contents

My name is Tina.

I like to dance.

Tap dancing is what
I do best.

I wear special shoes to
tap-dance.

There are **metal taps**
on the bottoms
of the shoes.

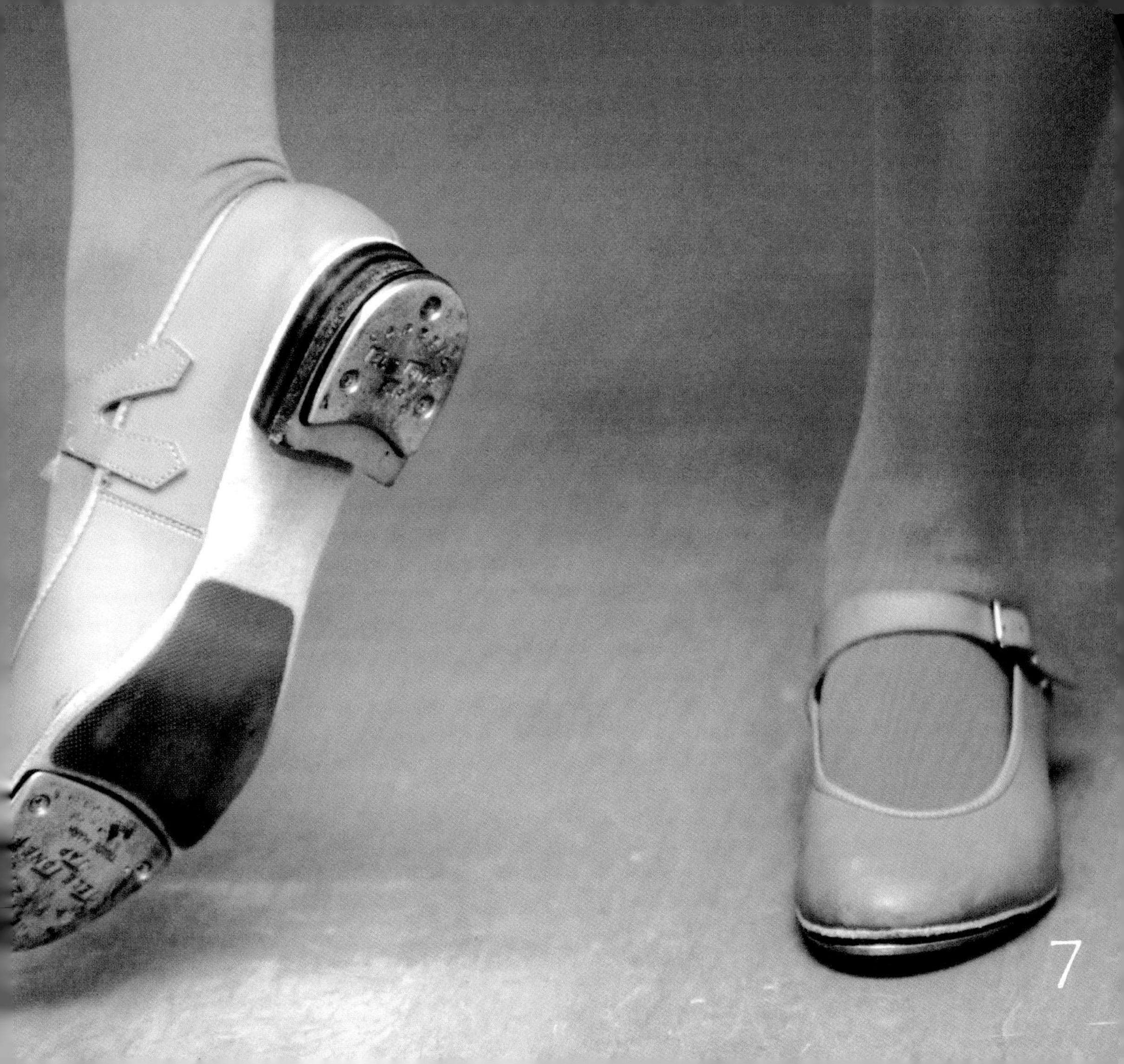

The shoes hit the floor and make tapping sounds.

That is why it is called tap dancing!

I go to tap-dancing class.

I learn **dance steps** with my friends.

We **practice** our dance steps.

We stand in a row.

We watch the teacher.

We follow the teacher's dance steps.

EXIT

Today we learn a **jump**.

We jump into the air.

We land on the floor with both feet.

I also know the **cramp role**.

I jump up and land first on my toes.

Then my heels hit the floor.

After many weeks, we put on a show.

We dress up in **costumes**.

We dance on a **stage**.

We bow at the end of
the show.

We like tap dancing
for people.

New Words

costumes (**kos**-toomz) clothes worn for a show or party
cramp role (**kramp rohl**) a dance step in which the toes hit the floor before the heels
dance steps (**dans stepz**) the ways that feet move while dancing
jump (**jump**) a dance step in which you jump and have both feet hit floor at the same time
metal taps (**meh**-tl **taps**) pieces on the bottoms of shoes that make a tapping sound
practice (**prak**-tis) to do over and over
stage (**stayj**) an area above the floor where shows are put on

To Find Out More

Books

Tap Dancing at a Glance
by Jimmy Ormonde
Applewood Books

The Book of Tap
by Jerry Ames
David McKay Company

Web Site

The Hot Shot Tap Dancers
http://www.hotshottapdancers.com
Learn all about this talented family of tap dancers. This site includes bios of each dancer and pictures of the group. Check out the links to learn more about tap dancing.

Index

About the Author

Mark Thomas is a writer and an educator who lives in Florida.

Reading Consultants

Kris Flynn, Coordinator, Small School District Literacy, The San Diego County Office of Education

Shelly Forys, Certified Reading Recovery Specialist, W.J. Zahnow Elementary School, Waterloo, IL

Peggy McNamara, Professor, Bank Street College of Education, Reading and Literacy Program